Killer Whale Eyes

2019 Edition

Dallas & Rosa —
Haw'aa/Thank you for sharing
your kindness and love!
Your sis,
Sondra S. Segundo

Story & Art by

Sondra S. Segundo

Song: *Siigáay Gid Uu Díi Íijang - I Am A Child of the Ocean* composed & performed by Sondra S. Segundo.
Killer Whale Eyes Audiobook: Story told by author.
Recorded at Front Burner Studio in Seattle, Washington.

This book was funded in part by grants from Potlatch Fund, First People's Fund, Evergreen Longhouse, and Sealaska Heritage Institute.

For my elders, Uncle Miijuu, Auntie Viola, and Auntie Louise, who now live in the spirit realm. They were the last of their generation(s) of fluent speakers and clan matriarchs who spoke our dialect since birth. They helped in the creation of this book. Haw'aa/Thank you my dear uncle and sweet aunties for your love and wisdom.

Your legacy lives on.

INTRODUCTION

I created this whale tale from Haida stories that were passed down over the years. Our people have a powerful connection to the orca. This ancient relationship is reflected in our matrilineal clan system, regalia, art, songs and stories. We consider them family and treat these lives with honor and respect.

X̱áad kíl (Haida language) words used:

náanaa (grandma)

chanáa (grandpa)

dagwáang (dear one)

kún (whale)

jáadaas (girl)

síigaay (ocean)

gid (child)

díi (me)

íijang (to be)

hal (he, she, they)

hl (I)

gudánggang (feel)

SG̱áanaay (orca)

sG̱alangáay (song)

eehl (with)

kyáagaangs (to call, to call out)

kyáagaanggang (calling out)

Way back in time—about
423 years to be more exact—
in a Haida village by the sea,
a little girl was born with eyes
like no other.

Her eyes were unique and as blue as the ocean deep. When her beloved Haida people looked into these deep blue eyes, a feeling of quiet wonder came over them, like when you look out to sea on a warm summer day and know that the world is magic.

The little girl belonged to the Killer Whale House —one of many crest houses and clans in the village— and she loved to play in the water. As a young girl, her favorite playtime activity was swimming with the sea otters. She liked to hold the tiny babies in her hands.

She was so gentle and kind that the mama otters trusted her with their little ones. They, too, felt a quiet wonder when they looked into her eyes. During these alone times with her friends of the sea, she sang her song. It was a song that the people came to know and love, for it echoed the wondrous sounds of the ocean.

As she grew into a young
woman, her chanáa (grandpa)
taught her how to carve.
She showed amazing talent
in this skill.

Together, they worked on a very special canoe.

When the canoe was finished, the villagers
prepared for a potlatch celebration!

Everyone was so busy, they did not notice that their dagwáang (dear one) was not helping.

She was down by the water's edge, gazing at the canoe. Gradually, a warm feeling began to build inside her chest. She closed her eyes and imagined herself far from land, paddling strong and fast.

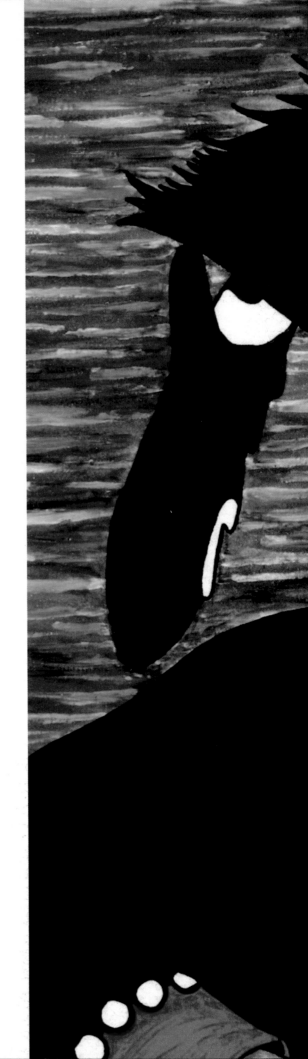

She opened her eyes and to her great surprise, she wasn't just imagining it! The village was ready to celebrate. They called out to their dagwáang—no answer. The canoe and the girl were gone.

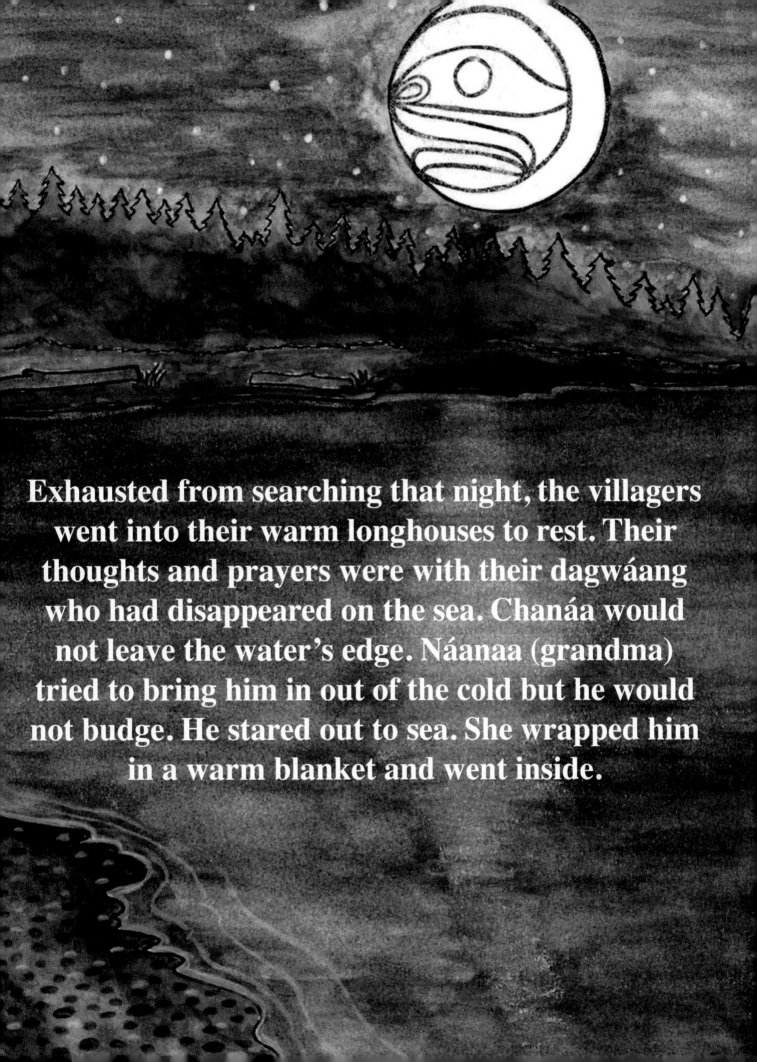

Exhausted from searching that night, the villagers went into their warm longhouses to rest. Their thoughts and prayers were with their dagwáang who had disappeared on the sea. Chanáa would not leave the water's edge. Náanaa (grandma) tried to bring him in out of the cold but he would not budge. He stared out to sea. She wrapped him in a warm blanket and went inside.

As the sun rose the next morning, chanáa was still waiting. His eyes were tired, and his body was chilled from the cool sea air. Suddenly, he saw the canoe! It was floating in with the tide! How happy he was! But when the canoe reached the shore, chanáa could see only her clothes and the paddle. She was not there.

Time passed as it always does—about four seasons to be more exact…Summer, Winter, Spring and Fall—yet the hearts of the people still ached. The people of the Killer Whale House decided to have a ceremony in honor of their dagwáang. Since her disappearance, the canoe had never been used. The people knew this was not right, so the canoe was once again carried to shore and launched. The people plunged their paddles into the water and were on their way. They paddled to the beat of chanáa's drumming and sang their dagwáang's special song…

Síigaay gid uu díi íijang

I am a child of the ocean

Díi hal kyáagaangs hl gudánggang

I hear her calling to me

SGáanaay gyaa sGalangáay eehl díi hal kyáagaanggang

Through the song of my relative killer whale

Díi hal kyáagaangs hl gudánggang

I hear her calling to me

Just then, a pod of killer whales surfaced. They, too, sang a song. It calmed the people. Slowly, the canoe drifted to a stop. The people and the whales had no fear of one another. They shared a peaceful love and respect.

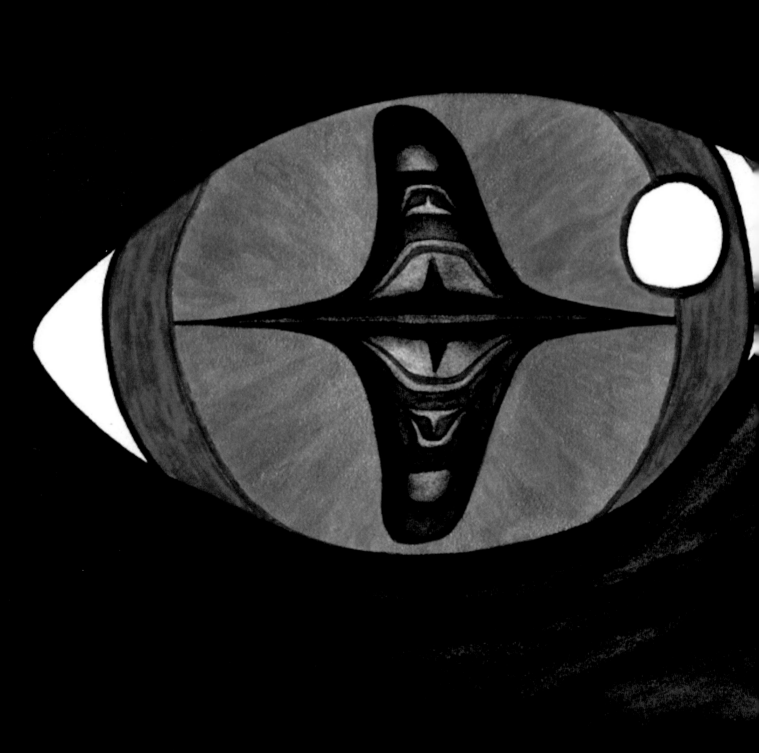

Chanáa looked into the eyes of one of the whales and saw that it was crying. He told the whale to come closer. They looked into each other's eyes and he understood that these were not tears of sadness, but of joy! In that moment, he realized that this whale had his granddaughter's beautiful eyes and spirit! It was their dagwáang! Oh, how their hearts were full of love and amazement as Kún Jáadaas (Whale Girl) greeted the people. How they had missed one another!

For you see, she was not lost after all; she had just joined her loved ones of the sea. And even though she had left her human life behind, Kún Jáadaas knew she and the Haida people would one day reunite. Although they lived in different worlds, they would always be close to help, comfort, and love each other. After all, family is family. Together, the people and the whales felt the ever so quiet wonder that told them the world is truly magic!

ACKNOWLEDGMENTS

I would like to give thanks to all who helped me in completing this book. Haw'aa to Saláanaa-Creator for healing me through art. To my children: Sorrel, Seri, and Shea, to whom I read my stories to over and over again until I got it right. Thank you for your patience and input. To my husband Eric Cunningham for helping me find my songs. To my parents and family for believing in me. To Sealaska Heritage Institute for helping to fund production of my book and publishing it. To Potlatch Fund, First People's Fund and Evergreen Longhouse for awarding me grant money to provide the tools and supplies needed. To my cousin, K'uyáang/Ben Young, who worked with the elders in our village to translate the words in my song into our Haida language. Finally, to all of our precious Haida elders for surviving and teaching us about our culture.

Haw'aa/Thank you!

ABOUT THE AUTHOR/ARTIST

Sondra S. Segundo-Cunningham is an artist and singer of the Haida language. She is an educator and has worked with youth in schools and programs throughout the Northwest, teaching art and sharing her Indigenous children's books and songs.

Everything Sondra does tells the story of her beloved people. All of her writings, song compositions, NW Coast Native art pieces, illustrations in her books, traditional dance, cultural teachings, language preservation work and community activism are all intertwined by her passion of reclaiming her Haida culture and sharing it from an Indigenous perspective.

Sondra grew up singing both traditional Haida songs with elders and gospel music in a church choir. She brings both worlds together while singing with tribal-funk band, Khu.eex' as lead female vocals. Sondra also released her first album,
Díi Gudangáay uu Síigaay - I Can Feel the Ocean in 2018.

As long time drum and dance leader for the Haida Heritage Foundation dance group, she raised funds to help start the Haida Roots Language and Youth Arts program for her community. This program is creating space for Seattle based Haida to practice traditional art-forms and re-learn their critically endangered X̱áad Kíl (Haida language) through structured learning from local Haida elders, traditional artists and teachers.

Audiobook and music download: Store.cdbaby.com/Artist/SondraSSegundo

SondraSegundo.com - Facebook.com/SondraSegundo/ - Instagram.com/SondraSegundo/

Made in the USA
San Bernardino, CA
26 February 2020